Dad went to the building site. He took Wilf and Wilma.

They looked at the crane.

Wilma spoke to the man in the cab.

A van came to the building site.

It had a weather vane on
the back.

Wilf looked at the weather vane.

Dad had an idea.

Wilf jumped over the weather vane.

"Be careful," said Dad.

"Take a photograph," said Wilma.

She jumped over the weather vane.

The weather vane went on the roof.

Wilf took a photograph.

"See the weather vane," said Wilf.
"We've jumped over it," said Wilma.

"What a tall story!" said Biff.

But Wilf had a photograph.
"See," he said.